THIS WALKER BOOK BELONGS TO:

_____

_____

_____

_____

I like...

thunder and lightning

I hate...

being a pair

people who stare

having to share

For Maria and Joe

First published 1991 by
Walker Books Ltd
87 Vauxhall Walk
London SE11 5HJ

This edition published 1993

4 6 8 10 9 7 5

Printed in Hong Kong

British Library Cataloguing in Publication Data
A catalogue record for this book is
available from the British Library.
ISBN 0-7445-3019-9

What I like

Catherine and Laurence Anholt

WALKER BOOKS

AND SUBSIDIARIES

LONDON • BOSTON • SYDNEY

What I like is...

time to play

a holiday

toys

(some) boys

waking early

hair all curly

What we like is…

jumping about

having a shout

going out

I don't like...

getting lost

I love...

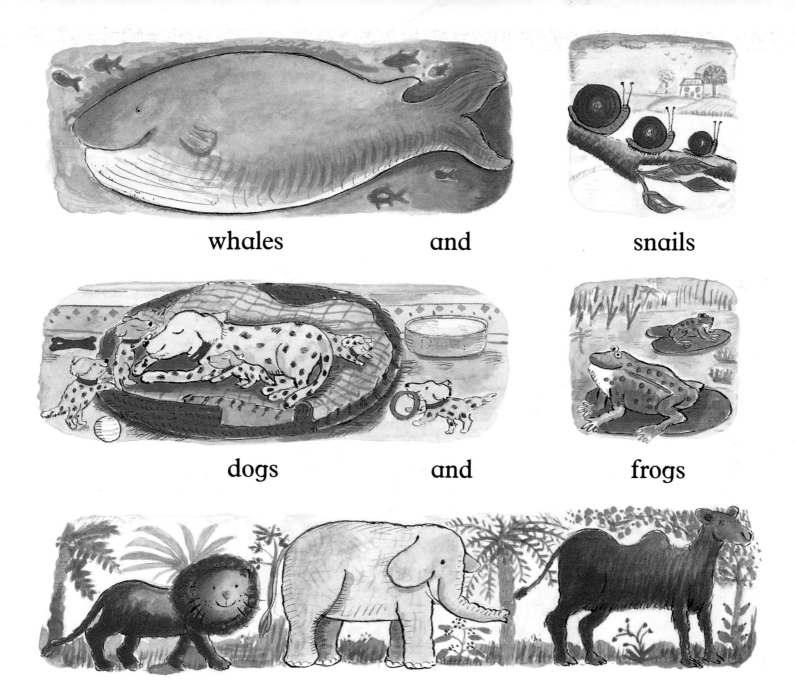

whales   and   snails

dogs   and   frogs

lots of animals

Sometimes we don't like…

playing with my mother

and my new baby brother

What I like is...

ice-cream

a funny dream

my thermos flask

my monster mask

I love...

playing the fool   a swimming pool   nursery school

I don't like…

fleas

peas

bees

aches

snakes

breaks

bumps

lumps

dumps

rats

gnats

bats

What we all like is...

a Christmas tree

watching TV

a place to hide

a pony ride

let's pretend

a happy end and . . .

Making a friend.

MORE WALKER PAPERBACKS
For You to Enjoy

KIDS
by Catherine and Laurence Anholt

A comprehensive, beautifully observed warts-and-all rhyming guide to kid kind.

0-7445-2011-3   £3.99

WHEN I WAS LITTLE
by Marcia Williams

A series of intriguing comparisons between a child's life now and
what it was like, according to Granny, in her day.

"Delightful… Bright, detailed illustrations provide 2 to 7-year-olds with lots to
look at and smile about, and the words are both simple and charming." *Practical Parenting*

0-7445-1765-6   £3.99

WORDS AND PICTURES
by Siobhan Dodds

A delightfully illustrated first picture dictionary of the familiar objects and activities of a toddler's life.

0-7445-2385-0   £3.99

Walker Paperbacks are available from most booksellers, or by post from B.B.C.S., P.O. Box 941, Hull, North Humberside HU1 3YQ

24 hour telephone credit card line 01482 224626

To order, send: Title, author, ISBN number and price for each book ordered, your full name and address,
cheque or postal order payable to BBCS for the total amount and allow the following for postage and packing:
UK and BFPO: £1.00 for the first book, and 50p for each additional book to a maximum of £3.50.
Overseas and Eire: £2.00 for the first book, £1.00 for the second and 50p for each additional book.

Prices and availability are subject to change without notice.